WELCOME TO THE ANCIENT FABUMOUSE WORLD OF THE MICEKINGS!

WHERE THEY LIVE: Miceking Island

CAPITAL: Mouseborg, home of the Stiltonord family

OTHER VILLAGES: Oofadale, village of the Oofa Oofa, and Feargard, village of the vilekings

CLIMATE: Cold, cold, cold, especially when the icy north wind blows!

TYPICAL FOOD: Gloog, a superstinky but fabumouse stew. The secret recipe is closely guarded by the wife of the miceking chief.

NATIONAL DRINK: Finnbrew, made of equal parts codfish juice and herring juice, with a splash of squid ink

MEANS OF TRANSPORTATION: The drekar, a light but very fast ship

GREATEST HONOR: The miceking helmet. It is only earned when a mouse performs an act of courage or wins a Miceking Challenge.

UNIT OF MEASUREMENT: A mouseking tail (full tail, half tail, third tail, quarter tail)

ENEMIES: The terrible dragons who live in Beastgard

Meet the Stiltonord Family . . .

GERONIMO
Advisor to the miceking chief

THEA
A horse trainer who works well with all kinds of animals

TRAP
The most famouse inventor in Mouseborg

BENJAMIN
Geronimo's nephew

BUGSILDA
Benjamin's best friend

. . . AND THE EVIL DRAGONS!

GOBBLER THE PUTRID
The fierce king of the dragons is a Devourer!

The dragons are divided into 5 clans, all of which are terrifying!

1. Devourers
They love to eat micekings raw — no cooking necessary.

2. Steamers
They grab micekings, then fly over volcanoes so the steam and smoke make them taste good.

SIZZLE
The cook

3. Biters
Before eating micekings, they nibble them delicately to see if they like them or not.

4. Slurpers
They wrap their long tongues around micekings and slurp them up.

5. Rinsers
As soon as they catch micekings, they rinse them in a stream to wash them off.

Geronimo Stilton

MICEKINGS
THE MYSTERIOUS MESSAGE

Scholastic Inc.

The publisher does not have any control over and does not assume any responsibility for author or third-party websites or their content.

Published by Scholastic Inc., *Publishers since 1920*, 557 Broadway, New York, NY 10012. SCHOLASTIC and associated logos are trademarks and/or registered trademarks of Scholastic Inc.

Stilton is the name of a famous English cheese. It is a registered trademark of the Stilton Cheese Makers' Association. For more information, go to www.stiltoncheese.com.

This book is a work of fiction. Names, characters, places, and incidents are either the product of the author's imagination or are used fictitiously, and any resemblance to actual persons, living or dead, business establishments, events, or locales is entirely coincidental.

ISBN 978-1-338-08872-4

Text by Geronimo Stilton
Original title *Nella terra degli Uffa Uffa*
Cover by Giuseppe Facciotto (pencils) and Flavio Ferron (ink and color)
Illustrations by Giuseppe Facciotto (pencils) and Alessandro Costa (ink and color)
Graphics by Chiara Cebraro

Special thanks to Tracey West
Translated by Emily Clement
Interior design by Kristine Brideson

10 9 8 7 6 5 4 3 2 1   17 18 19 20 21

Printed in the U.S.A.   40
First printing 2017

A Peaceful Evening for Geronimo!

It was a *peaceful* spring evening in Mouseborg, the capital city of Mouseking Island. The stars shone brightly in the sky. A gentle **breeze** blew in from the sea. Crickets chirped a soothing song.

Sorry, I should introduce myself: I am *Geronimo Stiltonord*, and I am a mouseking. Not a very fierce, fighting mouseking, but a scholarly one.

Chirp!
Chirp!
Chirp!

Ow, my back!

CRACK

And that night I had returned home after a terrible day!

1 During morning exercises, Sven the Shouter, our **Village chief**, had forced me to do 333 sit-ups!

2 At noon, dragons had attacked our village! They were looking to lunch on **FRESH MICEKING MEAT**. I fought

Narrow escape!

WOOSH

bravely (well, as bravely as I could. I have **WEAK** muscles for a mouseking). 3 And after that, my sister, Thea, had asked me to help her **rearrange** all the furniture in her house!

I was so tired that my **WHISKERS WERE DROOPING**!

So I was very happy to retreat to my house for a *peaceful*, quiet night. My plans included:

A light dinner of aged miceking cheese and herring soup . . .

Reading a book of **LEGENDS** about the famouse miceking **EXPLORER** Erik the Furry . . .

Ending with a SOOTHING cup of tea before bed . . .

I had just finished setting the table when I heard a knock at the door.

Bam! Bam! Bam!

Why, oh why, did someone always have to **INTERRUPT** me when I was eating?

As I peered through the peephole, I heard the **deep voice** of our village chief.

"**OPEN UP**, you smarty-mouseking! So says Sven!" he shouted.

A chorus of micekings behind him cried out,

"SO SAYS SVEN THE SHOUTER!"

Clattering cuttlefish! How many of them were out there? And what did they want from me?

"Well, **lazy bones**?" Sven yelled. "Are you going to open up?"

You should know that Sven is known as **THE SHOUTER** because he shouts very

loudly! And when he's angry, his shouts could make the walls of your house shake. So I hurried and opened the door before the chief could shout again.

A crowd of miceking warriors pushed into the house. They took seats in my chairs, on my tables, on my bed, and even in the rafters. Shivering squids, Sven had called a meeting of the Miceking Assembly in my house!

The warriors whispered to one another, "What could it be?" They were excited for a mystery to solve!

Then Sven spoke, "MICEKINGS OF MOUSEBORG, I have gathered you here for a matter of great importance."

The micekings listened in SILENCE, leaning forward in their seats.

Sven turned toward the foreman of the

STOCKER

Stocker is the foreman of the factory that makes finnbrew, the most popular miceking drink. He guards the barrels of finished finnbrew. He's a very slow-moving mouseking. When you ask him a question, he stares at you like a frozen codfish!

finnbrew factory. "Stocker! Tell us what you found."

Stocker looked **surprised**. "Me? Found? What?" **Great salty sardines**, what kind of mystery was this?

THE MYSTERIOUS JUG

Sven turned as **RED** as a pepper. "Stocker, stop acting like a **sea slug** and tell the others what you told me!"

"**SO SAYS SVEN THE SHOUTER!**" the micekings chanted.

"Hmm. Let's see," said Stocker. "Where should I start?"

"Start at the **BEGINNING**!" Sven demanded.

Stocker nodded. "Okay, then. I will start at the beginning," he said. "As you know, every night I take a walk around the outside of the factory."

"Yes, we know," Sven said **IMPATIENTLY**.

"I check to make sure that all the *barrels*

of finnbrew, left outside to ferment in the sun, have been brought inside," Stocker went on.

"By my beard, get on with the story!" Sven shouted. "At this rate, it will take you all night to tell it."

Stocker's fur was not ruffled. He kept talking. "So tonight, during my usual stroll, I NOTICED something floating in the water by the dock. So I walked over to get a better look, and . . ."

"AAAAAND?" all the micekings shouted, making my house SHAKE as if it were made of fjordberry jelly.

"And . . . I saw that it was an AMPHORA."

An amphora is a clay jug with two handles. But what was so important about Stocker finding a jug?

"I pulled it out of the water," he continued. "I opened it. And inside I found a . . ."

"Aaaaaaaa?" the micekings squealed.

"A parchment!" Stocker finished. "There was a *message* written on it, but I don't know how to read, so I ran to Sven."

"And I decided to come directly to Geronimo," Sven said. "Now read this *message*, smarty-mouseking. That's an order!"

"SO SAYS SVEN THE SHOUTER!"

Stocker handed me the parchment, and I began to read the message:

"I declare . . . to shake . . . um . . . strong mouseking! . . . sail the stormy seas . . . um . . . dragon . . . stinkiest . . . you . . ."

"Geronimo, quit **joking** around!" my cousin Trap exclaimed.

"I'm not **joking** around," I protested. "These are the only words I **UNDERSTAND**. I can barely make out two runes in a row!"

"You're supposed to be the **smarty-mouseking**!" Sven shouted. "Figure it out!"

"But, but, but . . ." I sputtered.

Trap took the parchment from my PAWS. "Leave it to me, cousin! In addition to being an INVENTOR, I'm also an expert at messages in bottles, secret codes, and invisible clues!"

Let's see . . .

Dear Sniffli,

... to ... all ... the ...
... ... I declare ... ...
... ...,
... ... to shake.
... ...,
... ... a strong mouseking!
... sail the stormy seas,
... ... dragon.
... ...
... ... stinkiest ...
... ... you ... ...
... ...

* The original letter was written in runes, the miceking alphabet. This is a translation for you readers!

Trap examined the parchment carefully (forward and BACKWARD, UP and DOWN, from close up and far away). Then he announced his conclusion: "**BRAVE** Sven! The amphora probably wasn't closed tightly. The salt water from the fjord has erased almost everything that was written here. And so . . . the original message is a mystery!"

A MESSAGE FROM YAN THE YAWNER

While Trap continued to study the message, our village chief paced the floor of my house, **muttering** about what to do next.

"HOLEY CHEESE!" Trap cried out suddenly. "What's this SEAL at the top of the parchment?"

"Let me see!" Sven yelled, grabbing the parchment from him. His eyes got wide.

"Why, this is the coat of arms of Yan

YAN
THE YAWNER

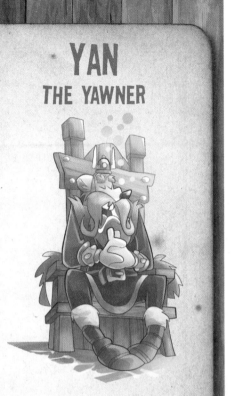

Yan the Yawner is the chief of Oofadale, where the Oofa Oofa live. He's called "the Yawner" because it's said he can yawn 1,007 times in a row without dislocating his jaw. His motto is, "Why do tomorrow what you can do next week?"

the Yawner, the chief of Oofadale!" Sven exclaimed.

"Salty sardines! Then this must be a message from him!" Trap said.

A **LOUD** murmur rose up from the micekings. This could be a very important message!

The micekings were jumping out of their FUR with curiosity. They started to **GUESS** what the meaning of the message might be, based on the few words I had read.

"Why, it's clear!" declared a tall, muscular mouseking. "It's a challenge sent by the Oofa Oofa! **THEY WANT TO ATTACK US!**"

"What if Oofadale is being attacked by **dragons**?" another mouseking wondered. "And Yan the Yawner is asking for help from the **strong**, **BRAVE** warriors of Mouseborg!"

A third mouseking spoke up. "They're insulting us! They think we're **stinky**!"

I had my own theory. "It could be that Yan was just writing a **simple** message of greeting to a **friend**," I suggested. "This very well could have been a **PERSONAL** letter that was **lost** and arrived here by accident. We all know how the miceking mail works . . ."

It's a challenge!
Is it a declaration of war?
It's an insult!
Um . . .
Hmm . . .
If you ask me . . .
They're asking for help!
What do we do?
I don't believe it!
I don't know!
No way!

But nobody took me SERIOUSLY.

"**By my beard**, Geronimo, you must be the most foolish smarty-mouseking in miceking history!" Sven scolded me. "Didn't you see the coat of arms? It's clearly an **official** message of some kind. Therefore we must respond in an **official** manner."

Sven paced the room, twirling his beard and thinking. The micekings eagerly waited to hear our chief's decision. Finally, Sven cleared his throat.

"If the village of **OOFADALE** is in danger, our miceking honor requires that we go help them!" Sven shouted. "And if they want to attack us, we must be ready to fight back with the strength of **Stenchberg cheese**! There is only one way to find out what the message really said. We will make an

official expedition to **OOFADALE**!"

"SO SAYS SVEN THE SHOUTER!"

Ready to go, smarty-mouseking?

Oh no!

All the micekings cheered with **joy** at this announcement. They hurried off to prepare for the expedition.

Everyone was excited . . . except me!

Great stinky clams, this journey could be risky, DANGEROUS, and PERILOUS!

And I . . . I was a scaredy-mouseking!

MISSION TO OOFADALE!

As soon as Sven said the word **expedition**, I tried to sneak off without being noticed. With everyone cheering, I had a good chance. I was only half a tail from the **door** when someone grabbed my shoulder.

I'm leaving!

It was Sven. "Geronimo, you **spineless jellyfish**, where do you think you're going?"

"W-w-well," I stuttered. "I just thought I'd go get us some more **finnbrew** and maybe a **snack**. Aren't you hungry?"

"I am hungry for *adventure*!" Sven replied. "We need to plan."

I tried again. "B-b-but . . . I left my **LAUNDRY** on the clothesline, and, um . . ."

"Stop BLABBERING, blubber head!" Sven shouted. "As smarty-mouseking of this village, and the OFFICIAL READER OF RUNES, you must be part of this expedition. Don't you want to finally earn your very first **miceking helmet**?"

I paused. A miceking helmet is the

greatest HONOR any mouseking can get. It is awarded to those who show great STRENGTH, courage, and Skill in battle. But my greatest strengths are in miceking HISTORY, rune grammar, and fjord GEOGRAPHY, and no helmet is awarded for those skills.

But if I did earn a **miceking helmet**,

then Sven's daughter, the beautiful **Thora**, might finally respect me!

With a far-off look, I *daydreamed* about my miceking crush. Trap snapped me out of it.

"Don't worry, cousin," he said. "I'll go with you on this mission!"

Great salty sardines, now I was really in **TROUBLE!** Every time my cousin Trap got involved, he usually tried out one of his crazy **inventions**. He has used me as his official test mouse, risking my **fur** every time!

"Why are you so excited to go on a miceking expedition?" I asked SUSPICIOUSLY.

"I'd like to see an old friend of mine in Oofadale, **Fen Whiskersson**," he explained. "We went to the **Young Miceking School for Inventors**

together when we were micelets.

"He's really nice," Trap continued. "I'm hoping to discuss some of my **new ideas** with him."

I groaned. **SHIVERING SQUIDS**, not another inventor! Now I'd have to deal with two of them. Who knew what **dangerous inventions** they would make me try out?

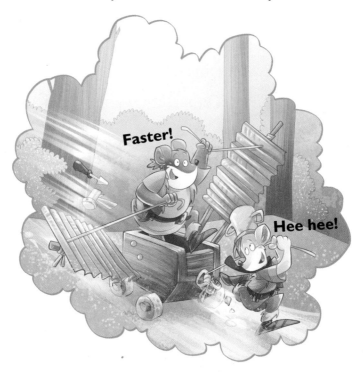

Squeak! I really didn't want to be a part of this miceking mission!

But I had no choice.

"I HaVe MaDe MY DeCiSiON!" Sven thundered. "Tomorrow we will **SET SAIL** for Oofadale at dawn. But I will not be leaving this mission in the clumsy paws of you two **CHeeSeHeaDS**." He pointed to Trap and me.

"You won't?" I asked.

"Of course not!" Sven shouted. "I will **lead** the mission. You two will accompany me. And we will need a team of ***brave warriors*** to go with us."

He started pointing to different micekings.

"You! Prepare the barrels of **finnbrew** and the crates of **anchovies**!" he ordered.

"You! Pack the wheels of **cheese**!

"You, you, and you, go shine the helmets and the shields!

"You, go polish the Mouseborg coat of arms until it glows like the sun! This expedition will be made in GRAND MICEKING STYLE!"

The micekings all replied together,

"SO SAYS SVEN THE SHOUTER!"

READY TO SET SAIL, BLUBBER HEADS?

I had trouble falling asleep that night. My whiskers *trembled* at the dangers we might encounter. **HOW, HOW, HOW** did I always end up in these situations?

When the **ROOSTER** crowed at dawn, I put my head under

Cock-a-doodle-doo!

the covers. I didn't want to go. I was a **SMARTY-MOUSEKING**, not a warrior!

Then I heard a **KNOCK** on my door. It was Trap.

"**GERONIMOOOO!** Come on, Cousin! It's time to begin our great mission!" he shouted.

I tried to get out of it. "Um, I can't find my boots anywhere. You go without me, and I'll meet up with you in Oofadale."

"I can tell when you're lying, Cousin," Trap said. "**Open the door!**"

I quickly thought of more excuses. "No, I woke up with a terrible **stomachache** and I have to run to the bathroom. And . . . **ACHOO!** I think I also caught a **MICEKING COLD**, and I don't want to get everyone sick!"

Trap still didn't believe me. "No more **EXCUSES**, Cousin. You don't want to make Sven **ANGRY**, do you?" he asked.

By my whiskers, I certainly didn't want to make our village chief angry! At the thought of Sven shouting at me, I got up and got dressed. As soon as I opened the door, Trap **GRABBED** me by the paw and D R A G G E D me along with

Get a move on!

him. He didn't even give me a chance to grab my **BACKPACK**!

"Let's hurry, Cousin! They're waiting for us!" Trap squealed.

He was right. When we reached

the port, we found micekings loading up two **drekars** for the long voyage. Others were rubbing the ships' hulls with CODFISH OIL.

I gazed up at the **towering** ships. Sven

commanded the *majestic* *Miceking Hero*. It was adorned with his official emblems. I tried to go on board, but a mouseking stopped me.

No room!

"**Halt!** There's no more room!" he said, holding up a paw. "Find another ship."

The next ship was the *Scourge of the North Sea*, with a *fearsome dragon* on its prow. But another mouseking stopped me there.

" **SCRAM**, smartymouseking. We're full! There's no more room!"

"Not even for a *small* mouseking like me?" I pleaded.

Scram!

Then Sven shouted from the prow of his ship,

"MICEKINGS, SET SAIL!"

Off we go!

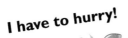

I have to hurry!

I had **ONE CHOICE** left . . . and I didn't like it! The only drekar left was the *Bated Breath*, the **shaky** tub that belonged to Olaf the Reckless.

And I get drekar-sick!

"Hop on board!" Olaf called out. "Don't

Oh no . . .

you want a *free ride*?"

I gave in and climbed on board. Then we
SET SAIL for Oofadale, the home of the
Oofa Oofa!

Hurry up, cabin boy!

DRAGON ATTACK!

Olaf put me to **WORK**. After I had organized our cheese supplies and **CLEANED** the deck, he sent me up to the main mast to be the lookout.

Me, who is AFRAID OF HEIGHTS!

The journey started off smoothly, and a breeze pushed us forward. After a while, though, the sky began to **darken**. A strange, oddly shaped **cloud** was floating toward us.

Was there a storm coming?

The cloud came closer . . . and **HOLEY CHEESE**, it wasn't a storm cloud at all! It was much worse!

"**Dragon attack!**" I shrieked.

The micekings on all three ships rushed to take up their shields, bows, and arrows. Four dragons **swooped** down on us. We could smell their swampy stink and see the SMOKE coming from their nostrils.

An orange dragon with a very, very long tongue licked his fangs.

"Purple Beard, look at all that fresh **miceking meat**!" he called out to his friend.

"You're right, Blue Tail!" the other dragon called back. "We could gobble one for a **SSS**nack and take the other**SSS** back to **Beastgard**!"

"Sizzle the cook make**SSS** a great miceking **SSS**tew!" said Blue Tail.

"I prefer them roa**SSS**ted," said Purple Beard.

Tasty!

Micekings!

Sven raised his fist in the air. "You won't get a taste of us, you **UGLY LIZARDS**! Micekings, **ATTACK**!"

All of the **MICEKINGS** threw themselves into the **BATTLE**, fighting off the dragons. Well, almost all. I stayed in the **CROW'S NEST**, so I wouldn't get in anybody's way.

Then the **LOOKOUT** on the *Scourge*

of the North Sea called out to me.

"Catch this *net*, smarty-mouseking!"

He **TOSSED** me one end of the net.

"This is no time to go **fishing**!" I called back.

But I **caught** the end of the net anyway, and it hung between the two ships.

We've got him!

Whoosh! A red dragon swooped down and flew right into it! He got all tangled up in the net!

"HOORAY! ONE DOWN!" the other lookout and I shouted.

Meanwhile, the **BATTLE** with the other dragons continued.

Yes!

I'm trapped!

Some micekings fought bravely with bows and arrows.

Others used LONG OARS to fend off the dragons.

Still others BLASTED them with jets of icy water from the North Sea. Everyone knows that dragons hate clean, cold water!

But as bravely as we fought, we were no match for the enormouse, strong dragons. And there, out in the OPEN OCEAN, we had no place to take shelter!

I scanned the horizon, looking for some sign of land.

I spotted a FOGGY patch of sky not far off. And as a scholarly mouseking, I knew that OOFADALE was almost always surrounded by fog.

Holey cheese, we were close!

If we could make it to **SHORE**, we could take shelter and be *safe*! I had to think of something, fast!

FORWARD, MICEKINGS!

I quickly came up with a *fabumouse* plan: We could row at **TOP SPEED** until we were **HIDDEN** in the fog. But how could I let the others know? It wasn't easy to be heard over the **loud** sounds of battle. But I tried.

"**We must go into the fog!**" I shouted.

"Geronimo, don't be a **BLUBBER HEAD!** Now is not the time to **sit on a log**!" Sven shouted back. He had misunderstood me!

So I tried to act it out. I made ꝛowing motions with my arms.

"**By my beard!** This is not the time to

exercise, **smarty-mouseking**!" Sven shouted.
He just didn't get it!

I had to leave my safe perch. I
scurried down the mast and
found Olaf and Trap.

They don't understand!

I *quickly* explained my idea.

"GOOD THINKING, smarty-mouseking!" Olaf agreed.

We ran to the oars.

"**MICEKINGS, FULL SPEED AHEAD!**" Olaf commanded.

The *Bated Breath* bolted forward. The crews on the other two drekars guessed our plan and followed in our wake toward the FOG.

"What do those ta**SSS**ty mouthful**SSS** think they're doing?" Purple Beard asked.

"They won't e**SSS**cape u**SSS**!" said Blue Tail.

Purple Beard roared, "Follow them, fa**SSS**t!"

Luckily, though, the **north wind**

started to **BLOW** toward Oofadale, and helped us go even faster! Soon we were immersed in a **FOG** as dense as **ricotta cheese**.

"By my breath, I can't **SSS**ee a thing!" Blue Tail moaned.

"I think I **SSS**ee a drekar in front of me!" said Purple Beard. "Let me bla**SSS**t it with my *FIERY* breath!"

He shot a **BLAST** of flame into the fog.

"Hey!" cried Blue Tail. "You **SSS**corched my tail!"

Zzzzzzzzzz!
Zzzzzzzzzzz!

The dragons kept **BUMPING** into each other, and we kept sailing through the fog. Luckily, we quickly arrived at the port of Oofadale.

We tied up the drekars at the dock and set out in search of the village chief, **YAN THE YAWNER**.

We passed by many of the **OOFA OOFA**, but they were all asleep. They always nap in the **afternoon**. And in the morning time. And at noon . . . They are known for being very **SLEEPY** micekings!

"Where is **YAN THE YAWNER**?" Sven asked one of the Oofa Oofa.

OOFADALE: THE VILLAGE OF THE OOFA OOFA

OOFADALE is a village on the southern coast of Miceking Island. It is almost always engulfed in thick fog. It's a boring place where nothing ever (well, almost ever) happens.

The micekings in this village call themselves the Oofa Oofa. They're generally very sleepy and don't get much done during the day. Their official cheese is Sluggozola, which takes a long, long, long, long time to ripen.

"ANSWER SVEN THE SHOUTER!"

the micekings yelled.

The villager *yawned* in response. Then he closed his eyes and fell **asleep** standing up!

We kept walking until we got to **Snoozy Square,** the village center. Sven walked up to another Oofa Oofa.

Zzzz!

"Tell me where I can find your **village chief**!" he barked.

But this Oofa Oofa was sleeping, too, and didn't wake up.

Furious, Sven stomped to a small building in the middle of the square. I read the runes above the window: OOF OOF OOF. That stands for THE OFFICIAL TOURIST OFFICE OF OOFADALE.

Sven pounded his fist on the counter. "**SHIVERING SQUIDS**, do you know who I am?" he shouted at the sleeping rodent working there. "I ORDER you to tell me right now where I can find Yan the Yawner, or **I'll have your fur**!"

I wouldn't have wanted to be in the place of that Oofa Oofa, When Sven gets ANGRY, his loud voice can curl your whiskers!

The rodent opened his eyes very, very slowly.

Then he opened his mouth very, very, slowly, as though he were going to speak . . .

Zzzz! Zzzz!

But he only snored.

Then I **NOTICED** something on the wall of the office.

"Chief, take a look at this sign!" I told Sven.

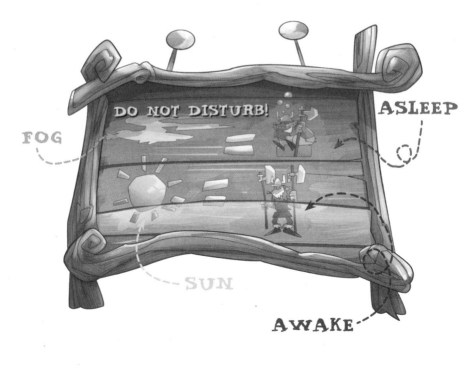

It suddenly made sense. When there's **FOG** in Oofadale (which is most of the time), the villagers take a miceking nap!

"There's **NO TIME** to waste!" Sven shouted. "As soon as the fog lifts, the dragons will attack. **WE MUST WAKE UP THESE CHEESEHEADS!**"

WAKE UP! WAKE UP! WAKE UUUUUP!

Sven began to **SHOUT** orders at all of the **MICEKINGS** from Mouseborg.

"Geronimo and Trap! Go **FIND** Yan the Yawner!"

"Wh-wh-why us?" I stammered.

Sven gave me a **STERN** look. "Would you rather stay here and **FIGHT** the dragons, smarty-mouseking?" he asked.

I didn't **wait** for him to change his mind. I grabbed my cousin and **DRAGGED** him back toward the tourist office. We had to find out where **YAN THE YAWNER** was!

Behind us, Sven continued to SHOUT orders.

"You, wake up the sleeping Oofa Oofa! You, take the young micekings in this village to safety! The others, come with me!"

Meanwhile, I stared at the sleeping Oofa Oofa at the counter of the tourist office. I had no idea how to wake him up!

"I've Got tHiS, CoUSin," Trap said.

Then he clapped his paws right next to one of the ears of the napping rodent!

Clap! Clap! Clap!

The rodent opened his eyes.

"Oofa! Didn't you (yawn) read the sign (yawn)? When there is fog in (yawn) Oofadale, it's time for a (yawn) miceking nap," he slowly complained.

HOW TO WAKE A SLEEPING OOFA OOFA

Whenever the fog rolls in, the Oofa Oofa start napping wherever they happen to be: on the street, at the market, or even in the bathroom. There are only three ways to wake them:

1 With a loud noise!

2 With a dose of fresh fruit to the head!

CLAP

BONK!

HA HA HA HA!

3 By tickling their feet!

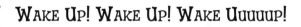

"Please excuse my cousin's manners," I said. "But this a SUPER-MICEKING EMERGENCY!"

The Oofa Oofa did not move a whisker at this news.

"We must find Yan the Yawner *immediately*!" I shrieked.

The rodent very, very slowly opened his mouth again.

"Take Oofwood Road (yawn) to Oofson Way and make a right (yawn)," he said. "Then take the second right (yawn), cross the bridge, and turn onto the first street (yawn) on the left. The (yawn) fifth house on the right is Yan's. Got it?"

"Um . . . we HOPE so!" Trap and I replied.

"You won't (yawn) find him awake," the Oofa Oofa told us. "It's nap time."

"He has to wake up! **IT'S AN EMERGENCY!**"
I exclaimed.

Trap nudged me. "Hey, do you think we should ask this rodent about the mysterious **letter** we found in the amphora?"

Yaawn!

When the Oofa Oofa heard this, he suddenly LIT UP. "Did you say letter? Hidden in an amphora?"

But I was already **PULLING** Trap away. "We'll worry about that later! Right now, we have to **save** your village from an army of *ferocious* dragons!"

As we **RAN OFF** to find Yan, we heard a **strange alarm** ring through the village.

Yaaawn! Yaaawn! Yaaawn!

It was Oofadale's **dragon alarm**!

That meant the dragons were close by. Trap and I had to hurry, or else . . .

. . . WE COULD BECOME A DRAGON'S DINNER!

Ruuuuuun!

The fog was lifting and the dragons had spotted Oofadale! **Hungry** for miceking meat, they **SPED** toward the village. There was no time to lose!

Sven pointed to one of the napping Oofa Oofa. "**Wake up**, lazybones! Tell us where the catapults are, quick, or we'll all be **toasted** like grilled cheese sandwiches!"

Without opening his eyes, the rodent **POINTED** to a large

building on the other side of the square. Sven and the micekings **raced** inside.

"**By my beard!** These catapults are dusty, RUSTY, and covered in cobwebs!" Sven exclaimed.

Then he frowned. "Let's move them out! We have to at least try."

The micekings of Mouseborg **dragged** the **HEAVY** catapults out into the square. By that time, the dragons were overhead.

"Now is the moment, my B O L D and **brave** micekings," Sven shouted. **"GET READY TO ATTACK!"**

"Chief, we need **rocks**!" one of the micekings said.

"You mean the catapults

Zzzz zzzz!

Zzzz!

Zzzz . . . .

aren't loaded?" Sven asked. "Oofa Oofa, where are your rocks?"

Zzzzzzzz. The Oofa Oofa were still all napping!

By now the **dragons** were so close, the micekings could smell their **horrible** breath.

"There's only one thing to do," Sven said.

To the catapults!

Run!

"RUUUUUUUN!"

The dragons looked down on the village, confused. Some of the micekings (from Mouseborg) were **RUNNING** back and forth, looking for rocks. But other micekings (from Oofadale) were **fast asleep**!

"Why are they **SSS**leeping?" a green dragon asked. "Don't they fear u**SSS**?"

SAVED BY INVENTION!

While Sven and our fellow miceking warriors faced the dragons' attack, Trap and I searched for the house of Yan the Yawner.

We made a right on Oofa Road. Or was it Oofa Way? Then we made two LEFTS . . . and one right . . . and soon we were as LOST as two anchovies in the big sea!

"We were supposed to go LEFT back there, Cousin!" Trap said.

"No, I'm sure we were supposed to go right after the bridge!" I argued. "And then make another right? Or was it a LEFT?"

Great moldy mussels, I

couldn't remember!
And while Trap
and I stood there,
scratching our
heads, a threatening
shadow crept up
over us. We looked up and
GASPED!

Purple Beard and Blue Tail, those two
hungry dragons, had found us!

"**SSS**niff, **SSS**niff," Purple Beard hissed.
"Do you **SSS**mell the ta**SSS**ty aroma of fresh
micekings? It **SSS**mell**SSS** familiar . . ."

"Ye**SSS**! Look!" Blue Tail exclaimed. "It's that SHRIMPY mouseking who **SSS**ailed away from u**SSS** before!"

"Run, Cousin!" Trap shouted.

I darted after him. He looked over his shoulder.

"Let's SPLit up to confuse them!" he yelled.

"Wh-why? I don't want to be alone!" I yelled back.

But Trap was already heading in the opposite direction.

"That mouseking is mine!" Purple Beard shouted, and he flew after Trap.

But the dragon wasn't used to flying so low. When he turned the corner to follow Trap, he didn't see the big WOODEN AND IRON sign for the Oofadale blacksmith.

Baaaaam!

He flew into it, smashing his face as FLAT as a flounder!

Meanwhile, I was running as fast as I could. But I ran right into a dead end! When I turned, I saw Blue Tail flying right at me, with his jaws open wide!

Shivering squids, I was as good as fried! I closed my eyes, waiting for the worst.

All of a sudden I heard

Ow!

Trap's voice. "Hey, Cousin! Check this out!"

I opened my eyes and saw that Trap had strange springs attached to his feet. He was wearing SPRING STEPPERS!

"HURRY, jump on!" he urged.

"I don't think so, Trap! Are you sure those things are S-S-SAFE?" I stuttered.

Then Blue Tail launched a

Trust me!

Squeak!

FIREBALL at me, and I didn't wait for Trap's answer. I jumped on, and Trap quickly bounced away.

Boing! Boing!

Boing!

SPRING STEPPERS

This invention adds a *bounce* to your step! Thanks to the springs on the bottoms of these shoes, it's possible to jump as high as ten miceking tails. **THESE ARE NOT RECOMMENDED FOR MICEKINGS WHO ARE AFRAID OF HEIGHTS!**

No Time for Tea!

Many bounces later (**SQUEAK!** I was getting motion sick!), we arrived at the home of Yan the Yawner, the village chief. Inside we saw two Oofa Oofa, dozing in armchairs.

"Greetings, Oofa friends," I said. "My **name** is Geronimo Stiltonord, and this is my cousin Trap."

Zzzzzzzzz.

"We are sorry to wake you, but

Help!

How fun!

Fen Whiskersson

Fen is the official inventor in the village of Oofa Oofa. He attended the Young Miceking School for Inventors with Trap. The contraptions he invents are inspired by the dreams he has while napping!

we have come all the way from Mouseborg on an IMPORTANT matter," I continued, but Trap interrupted me.

"Fen Whiskersson, is that you?" he cried. He **clapped** his paws next to one of the sleeping rodents.

The mouse's eyes fluttered open. "Trap, my old inventing buddy, is that really you?"

"It sure is!" Trap replied. The two old friends hugged.

"What good **north wind** brings you to Oofadale?" Fen asked.

"As my cousin said, we're here on an IMPORTANT matter," Trap explained. "We need to see Yan the Yawner right away!"

The rodent in the other armchair began to stir. "**OOFA!** What's with all this racket? Don't you know it's nap time? Who is **disturbing** my slumber?"

At that moment, a third rodent entered the room, carrying a tray. "Who wants a cup of *tea?*"

"There is no time for tea!" I cried, but then I stopped. "Hey, aren't you the **OOFA OOFA** from the tourist office?"

"Correct!" he replied. "My name is Bronk Snorborg."

Then Bronk whispered in my ear. "I'm glad you **finally** got here," he said. "We

really need to talk about that letter you told me about earlier. The one you found in the amphora."

"We can talk about the letter later!" I blurted out. "Right now, we have important news! **Dragons are attacking Oofadale!**"

The other Oofa straightened up in his chair. "Holey cheese! Why didn't you say that IMMEDIATELY?" he cried.

"Are you Yan the Yawner?" I asked.

"Yes, I am!" he said, squinting at me. "And are you sure you're from Mouseborg? Micekings there are usually very **tall** and strong. You seem very short and softer than a jellyfish."

"And where is your MICEKING HELMET?" Fen asked me.

So many unnecessary questions! These two

rodents were really getting under my fur!

"Great salty sardines!" I shrieked in exasperation. "There is no time to explain! The dragons are attacking.

DON'T YOU HAVE A DRAGON DEFENSE PLAN IN OOFADALE?"

ESSENCE OF SEA JASMINE

Fen the inventor and **YAN** the Yawner talked privately for a few minutes. Then Fen motioned for Trap and me to follow him. He led us to a **SMALL HUT** nearby.

"Welcome to my laboratory!" he exclaimed as he opened the door for us. "It is here that I create my **GENIUS** inventions. If the **answer** to our dragon problem is anywhere, it will be here."

Inside the hut was what looked like a great big pile of **junk**.

Fen dove into the **MOUNTAIN** of junk and started rummaging around.

"Tell me what you're **LOOKING** for, old friend, and I'll help you find it,"

Trap offered.

"It's obvious!" Fen replied. "I am looking for my FABUMOUSE invention designed to defend Oofadale from dragons: **THE WIND CYCLE**!"

Trap and I shared a confused look. We had no idea what he was talking about!

Then Fen extracted a *strange-looking* contraption from the pile. It had a wheel with two pedals.

"EUREKA!" he cried. "Found it!

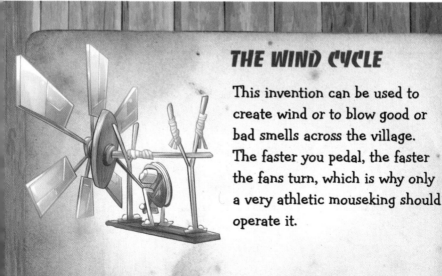

THE WIND CYCLE

This invention can be used to create wind or to blow good or bad smells across the village. The faster you pedal, the faster the fans turn, which is why only a very athletic mouseking should operate it.

And in this little bottle is essence of sea jasmine!"

I sniffed it. "It smells very clean! What's it for?"

"We will use the Wind Cycle to spread the scent of sea jasmine over the whole village," Fen replied.

"**I get it!**" Trap exclaimed. "Dragons hate clean smells. It will drive them away."

"Exactly!" Fen said.

"So where is the highest point in Oofadale?" I asked.

Fen went to the window and pointed. "The top of Mount Mattress!"

I looked out the window and saw only a **small hill**.

"But that's just a tiny hill," I said.

"But that's the highest mountain in all of Oofadale!" Fen said, sounding offended. "The Wind Cycle must be taken to the very top of the pine tree that grows on the mountain's peak."

I started to get a **BAD FEELING**. "And who,

There's Mount Mattress!

exactly, will take it there?" I asked.

"It's obvious!" Fen said. "You need to get a miceking helmet, don't you? Well, here is the perfect chance to earn one. Good luck **DODGING** those dragons on your way!"

Clammering clams, I had a **tRUe miceKiNG missioN** ahead of me!

PEDAL, GERONIMO!

Trap and I walked along the path that led to the PEAK of Mount Mattress, the tallest . . . *hill* in Oofadale!

We carried Fen's VERY HEAVY invention with us. Or rather, I carried it. Trap carried the tiny bottle of sea jasmine essence and a roll of *parchment* with instructions for using the Wind Cycle.

"Couldn't we . . . PUFF . . . trade . . . pant?" I asked.

"What kind of MOUSEKING are you?" Trap asked. "Use your miceking muscles, Cousin!"

Finally, we arrived at the base of the pine tree. I started to **CLIMB** up the ladder to get to the top, but . . .

Puff . . . pant . . .

Faster!

1. First I stepped on some mountain eagle poo. BLECH!

2. Then I lost my footing, slipped, and fell on some sharp pine needles. OUCH!

3. I slipped again and smacked my snout on a branch. SQUEAK!

Finally, I reached the **observation** platform at the top of the tree. From there, I could see the WHOLE VILLAGE of Oofadale!

"Get on the Wind Cycle and PEDAL, GERONIMO!" Trap called up to me.

I had to act fast. I hopped on the seat and started to pedal *fast . . . faster . . . even faster*!

What a workout!

My tired legs were starting to feel like STRiNg Cheese!

Aim . . .

Trap emptied the essence of sea jasmine in front of the fan, and the wind spread the scent all over Oofadale.

Down below, we could

Attack!

Take that, lizard face!

see the brave micekings **battling** the dragons. The Oofa Oofa had finally woken up from their naps and joined the **warriors** from Mouseborg.

"Where is that smarty-mouseking?" **SVEN** shouted, hurling a **hammer** at a green dragon. "He was supposed to bring more help!"

Just missed!

"**WATCH OUT, CHIEF!**" Olaf shrieked.

The hammer missed the green dragon. The **ANGRY** dragon grabbed Sven by the tail.

"Now to **GOBBLE** you up!" the dragon said. Then he suddenly sneezed. "**ACHOO!**"

The dragon dropped Sven.

What happened?

In less time than it takes to eat a cheese cracker, all of the dragons were in tears. "**Hammering herrings**, what's happening?" Olaf asked. "Why are the dragons crying?"

The green dragon began to wail. "What is**SSS** that terrible **SSS**mell?" he asked. "I can't keep my eye**SSS** open!"

"It's too clean!" whined a red dragon. "I **SSS**mell soap! And flower**SSS**! And I can't **SSS**top **SSS**neezing! **ACHOO!**"

"Fen was right!" I told Trap. "The dragons can't stand the **SUPER-clean** smell of the sea jasmine."

The dragons beat a quick retreat, flying off into the clouds one after another.

From the top of the pine tree, Trap and I watched as they fled, crying, sneezing, and swerving back and forth.

"It worked! We did it!" Trap and I cheered.
Then we happily ran toward the village. We
still had to figure where that letter came from.

THE SECRET OF THE LETTER

The miceking warriors **HUGGED** one another and cheered when the dragons flew away.

"Micekings work better when they fight together! Hip, hip, hooray! Hooray! Hooray!"

We did it!

Yan the Yawner hugged Sven. "Thank you for bringing that smarty-mouseking!" he said. "He really saved the day."

Then he turned to the rest of us. "Brave friends from Mouseborg, we thank you for your invaluable help today! We couldn't have done it without you. To celebrate, we will have a grand miceking feast!"

"SO SAYS YAN THE YAWNER!" chanted the Oofa Oofa.

Then Sven approached me. "Geronimo, this time you acted bravely, like a true mouseking," he said. "I have decided to award you with a miceking helmet."

WHAT, WHAT, WHAT? I couldn't believe my ears. At last I would receive my first miceking helmet!

My whiskers were shaking with excitement!

Well done, Geronimo!

Thank you!

"First, however," Sven continued, "I would like to find out at least what was written in that **MYSTERIOUS** letter from Yan the Yawner!"

Yan looked confused. "I didn't send a letter."

At that moment, Bronk Snorborg from the tourist office stepped forward.

"I think I can **solve** this mystery," he said.

Sven and Yan both shouted at once. "Speak! We order you!"

"**SO SAYS SVEN THE SHOUTER!**" chanted the Mouseborg warriors.

"**SO SAYS YAN THE YAWNER!**" chanted the Oofa Oofa.

Bronk cleared his throat. "Well, you see, I think it might be a love letter that I wrote for the lovely Snorina."

"**WHAAAAAAT?**" shouted Sven.

"A love letter?" yelled Yan.

Trap handed the letter to Bronk. "Is this it?"

"Yes!" Bronk cried *happily*.

"But why is the **official seal** of Oofadale on your letter?" Trap asked Bronk.

"Because I used one of the pieces of *parchment* that we use at the tourist

Dear Snorina,

You have stolen my heart,

and to you I declare all my love.

When I look at you,

my whiskers begin to shake.

With you by my side,

I could be a strong mouseking!

I could sail the stormy seas,

or slay the fiercest dragon.

For you I would climb the highest hill,

or eat the stinkiest cheese.

One smile from you is all I need,

but it would be nice if I had your love, too.

Bronk

* The original letter was written in runes, the miceking alphabet. This is a translation for you readers!

office to draw maps," Bronk admitted. "They all have the official coat of arms!"

I had a question, too. "Then why did you hide it in an **AMPHORA** and throw it into the sea?"

"That's not how it happened," Bronk answered. "You see, Snorina is the daughter of the Oofadale **MILKMAN**, and every evening she comes to collect the empty milk **BOTTLES**. I hoped that she would find my letter."

"So how did the amphora end up in the sea?" Trap wanted to know.

"That night there was a terrible storm!" Bronk replied. "A blast of wind must have carried the amphora to the dock, and then it rolled into the water."

Trap's eyes lit up. "Aha! Then the

current brought it to Mouseborg, where Stocker **found** it!"

Bronk nodded. "That must be what happened," he said, and then he turned to look at a lovely rodent who was **smiling** at him. "And all this time I thought that **Snorina** didn't return my feelings!"

Snorina stepped forward. "Oh, Bronk! If I had received the letter, I would have told you that **I feel the same way** about you."

Oh, Bronk!

"You mean the letter wasn't a **call for help**?" Sven fumed. "And you didn't want to **attack** our village? We arranged an official expedition in grand miceking style just for a **love letter**?"

"It looks that way," Bronk said.

"Why didn't you tell us this as **SOON** as we arrived?" Sven shouted.

Bronk pointed at me. "I did try to tell someone—that shrimpy mouseking over there."

Uh-oh. This was not going to be good.

"Is this **TrUe**, Geronimo?" Sven asked me.

"W-w-well, yes," I stammered. "B-b-but the **dragons** were attacking, and . . ."

"You **cHeeSeHeaD**!" Sven shouted. "First, you **FAILED** to figure out the letter. Then, you could have found out it was just a *love letter*, but you didn't listen.

NO MICEKING HELMET FOR YOU!"

"B-b-but the dragons . . ." I tried to explain.

"Enough of this. It's time for the **feast**!"
Yan yelled.

"**SO SAYS YAN THE YAWNER!**"
cheered all the micekings.

Everyone ate and talked and laughed. I sat outside all ALONE, thinking about the miceking helmet that I had WON and LOST in a matter of minutes. Would I ever be able to show Thora that I was a truly brave mouseking?

Then Bronk and Snorina approached me.

"Thank you for bringing the letter back to us, Geronimo," Bronk said. "It brought Snorina and me together."

"Even without a helmet, you are **VeRy BRaVe**," she said. "One day you will win over your own miceking love, I'm sure."

I smiled. "Thank you," I said. "I know one day I will finally get my miceking helmet!"

But that's another miceking story, for another miceking time!

MICEKING ISLAND

Beastgard

Gullet Valley

Feargard

Forest of a
Thousand
Scales

Oofadale

Helpful Hills

Yawning
Cove

Mouseborg

Don't miss any adventures of the Micekings!

#1 Attack of the Dragons

#2 The Famouse Fjord Race

#3 Pull the Dragon's Tooth!

#4 Stay Strong, Geronimo!

#5 The Mysterious Message

Up Next:

#6 The Helmet Holdup

Be sure to read all my fabumouse adventures!

#1 Lost Treasure of the Emerald Eye

#2 The Curse of the Cheese Pyramid

#3 Cat and Mouse in a Haunted House

#4 I'm Too Fond of My Fur!

#5 Four Mice Deep in the Jungle

#6 Paws Off, Cheddarface!

#7 Red Pizzas for a Blue Count

#8 Attack of the Bandit Cats

#9 A Fabumouse Vacation for Geronimo

#10 All Because of a Cup of Coffee

#11 It's Halloween, You 'Fraidy Mouse!

#12 Merry Christmas, Geronimo!

#13 The Phantom of the Subway

#14 The Temple of the Ruby of Fire

#15 The Mona Mousa Code

#16 A Cheese-Colored Camper

#17 Watch Your Whiskers, Stilton!

#18 Shipwreck on the Pirate Islands

#19 My Name Is Stilton, Geronimo Stilton

#20 Surf's Up, Geronimo!

#21 The Wild, Wild West

#22 The Secret of Cacklefur Castle

A Christmas Tale

#23 Valentine's Day Disaster

#24 Field Trip to Niagara Falls

#25 The Search for Sunken Treasure

#26 The Mummy with No Name

#27 The Christmas Toy Factory

#28 Wedding Crasher

#29 Down and Out Down Under

#30 The Mouse Island Marathon

#31 The Mysterious Cheese Thief

Christmas Catastrophe

#32 Valley of the Giant Skeletons

#33 Geronimo and the Gold Medal Mystery

#34 Geronimo Stilton, Secret Agent

#35 A Very Merry Christmas

#36 Geronimo's Valentine

#37 The Race Across America

#38 A Fabumouse School Adventure

#39 Singing Sensation

#40 The Karate Mouse

#41 Mighty Mount Kilimanjaro

#42 The Peculiar Pumpkin Thief

#43 I'm Not a Supermouse!

#44 The Giant Diamond Robbery

#45 Save the White Whale!

#46 The Haunted Castle

#47 Run for the Hills, Geronimo!

#48 The Mystery in Venice

#49 The Way of the Samurai

#50 This Hotel Is Haunted!

#51 The Enormouse Pearl Heist

#52 Mouse in Space!

#53 Rumble in the Jungle

#54 Get into Gear, Stilton!

#55 The Golden Statue Plot

#56 Flight of the Red Bandit

The Hunt for the Golden Book

#57 The Stinky Cheese Vacation

#58 The Super Chef Contest

#59 Welcome to Moldy Manor

The Hunt for the Curious Cheese

#60 The Treasure of Easter Island

#61 Mouse House Hunter

#62 Mouse Overboard!

The Hunt for the Secret Papyrus

#63 The Cheese Experiment

#64 Magical Mission

#65 Bollywood Burglary

The Hunt for the Hundredth Key

#66 Operation: Secret Recipe

#67 The Chocolate Chase

Don't miss any of my special edition adventures!

THE KINGDOM OF FANTASY

THE QUEST FOR PARADISE:
THE RETURN TO THE KINGDOM OF FANTASY

THE AMAZING VOYAGE:
THE THIRD ADVENTURE IN THE KINGDOM OF FANTASY

THE DRAGON PROPHECY:
THE FOURTH ADVENTURE IN THE KINGDOM OF FANTASY

THE VOLCANO OF FIRE:
THE FIFTH ADVENTURE IN THE KINGDOM OF FANTASY

THE SEARCH FOR TREASURE:
THE SIXTH ADVENTURE IN THE KINGDOM OF FANTASY

THE ENCHANTED CHARMS:
THE SEVENTH ADVENTURE IN THE KINGDOM OF FANTASY

THE PHOENIX OF DESTINY:
AN EPIC KINGDOM OF FANTASY ADVENTURE

THE HOUR OF MAGIC:
THE EIGHTH ADVENTURE IN THE KINGDOM OF FANTASY

THE WIZARD'S WAND:
THE NINTH ADVENTURE IN THE KINGDOM OF FANTASY

THE SHIP OF SECRETS:
THE TENTH ADVENTURE IN THE KINGDOM OF FANTASY

THE DRAGON OF FORTUNE:
AN EPIC KINGDOM OF FANTASY ADVENTURE

THE JOURNEY THROUGH TIME

BACK IN TIME:
THE SECOND JOURNEY THROUGH TIME

THE RACE AGAINST TIME:
THE THIRD JOURNEY THROUGH TIME

LOST IN TIME:
THE FOURTH JOURNEY THROUGH TIME

Don't miss any of these exciting Thea Sisters adventures!

Thea Stilton and the
Dragon's Code

Thea Stilton and the
Mountain of Fire

Thea Stilton and the
Ghost of the Shipwreck

Thea Stilton and the
Secret City

Thea Stilton and the
Mystery in Paris

Thea Stilton and the
Cherry Blossom Adventure

Thea Stilton and the
Star Castaways

Thea Stilton: Big Trouble
in the Big Apple

Thea Stilton and the
Ice Treasure

Thea Stilton and the
Secret of the Old Castle

Thea Stilton and the
Blue Scarab Hunt

Thea Stilton and the
Prince's Emerald

Thea Stilton and the
Mystery on the Orient Express

Thea Stilton and the
Dancing Shadows

Thea Stilton and the
Legend of the Fire Flowers

Thea Stilton and the
Spanish Dance Mission

Thea Stilton and the
Journey to the Lion's Den

Thea Stilton and the
Great Tulip Heist

Thea Stilton and the
Chocolate Sabotage

Thea Stilton and the
Missing Myth

Thea Stilton and the
Lost Letters

Thea Stilton and the
Tropical Treasure

Thea Stilton and the
Hollywood Hoax

Thea Stilton and the
Madagascar Madness

Thea Stilton and the
Frozen Fiasco

And check out my fabumouse special editions!

THEA STILTON:
THE JOURNEY
TO ATLANTIS

THEA STILTON:
THE SECRET OF
THE FAIRIES

THEA STILTON:
THE SECRET OF
THE SNOW

THEA STILTON:
THE CLOUD
CASTLE

THEA STILTON:
THE TREASURE
OF THE SEA

Dear mouse friends,
thanks for reading,

and good-bye until
the next book!